HARVEY MILK:

NO

TO HOMOPHOBIA

HARVEY MILK:

NO

TO HOMOPHOBIA

SAFIA AMOR

Translated by RUTH DIVER

THEY SAID NO SERIES EDITOR, MURIELLE SZAC

TRIANGLE
SQUARE
books for young readers

an imprint of
Seven Stories Press
NEW YORK • OAKLAND • LONDON

Seven Stories Press
www.sevenstories.com

Library of Congress Cataloging-in-Publication Data

Names: Amor, Safia, author. | Diver, Ruth, translator.
Title: Harvey Milk : no to homophobia / Safia Amor ; translated by Ruth
  Diver.
Description: Regular edition (rg). | New York City : Triangle Square Books
  for Young Readers / Seven Stories Press, [2022] | Series: They said no |
  Translated from French. | Includes bibliographical references. |
  Audience: Ages 10-14 years (1014) | Audience: Grades 7-9
Identifiers: LCCN 2022033855 | ISBN 9781644211847 (hardcover) | ISBN
  9781644211854 (ebook)
Subjects: LCSH: Social reformers--California--Biography--Juvenile
  literature. | Milk, Harvey--Juvenile literature. |
  Mayors--California--San Francisco--Biography--Juvenile literature. | Gay
  politicians--California--San Francisco--Biography--Juvenile literature.
  | Gay men--California--San Francisco--Biography--Juvenile literature. |
  Gay liberation movement--California--San Francisco--History--20th
  century--Juvenile literature.
Classification: LCC F869.S353 M54413 2022 | DDC 303.48/4092
  [B]--dc23/eng/20220715
LC record available at https://lccn.loc.gov/2022033855

Cover illustration: François Roca

College professors and high school and middle school teachers may order free
examination copies of Seven Stories Press titles. Visit https://www.sevenstories.
com/pg/resources-academics or email academics@sevenstories.com.

Printed in the USA.

9 8 7 6 5 4 3 2 1

For Jalil, Cyril, Alain, Martin,
Bertrand, Marc, Simon, Marine,
Patrice, Éric, Guillaume, Maxime...
Olivier, Timothée, Lucas, Mathieu...
Tiphaine, Lorine, Michèle, Assia, Agnès . . .
Marion, Maria and Murielle,
for saying yes to freedom.

"We will not
win our rights by staying
quietly in our closets."

Contents

1 August 1947   11

2 In the Navy   23

3 From Manhattan to San Francisco.   35

4 "My Name is Harvey Milk"   49

5 A Victory for Gay Rights   57

Afterword: They Too Said No   75

Chronology   87

For More Information   89

Discussion Questions   91

About the Author and Translator   91

1

August 1947

Harvey was lying on the grass in Central Park, looking up at the sky. A clear blue sky with dazzling sunbeams, on that early afternoon. Stretched out bare-chested and barefoot and wearing light cotton shorts, with his T-shirt rolled up as a pillow, Harvey was happy. He was finally going to start the novel that his grandfather had given him for his seventeenth birthday on May 22: *The Pearl*, by John Steinbeck, one of his favorite authors. Other men were also enjoying the beautiful summer's day, some gathered in groups on towels or blankets, others alone and sheltered from view, just as Harvey was. In the distance he could hear children's shouts coming from behind the boxwood hedges. As always on summer Sundays, families were spending the whole day in the park—the city's lungs, where the air was more breathable than in the crowded streets of New York. They must be running around the Bethesda Fountain, having fun splashing each other, Harvey thought, remembering the many times his mother Minnie had taken him and his brother Bob to the park near their house. All his neighborhood friends would make water pistols with bottles and run around spraying each other. He remembered how he particularly liked water bombing Bill, that chubby guy who was always making fun of Dick, the only Black boy that played in the park with them. Harvey didn't like Mary either, that little goody-two-shoes who screamed as soon as he touched her, when he really didn't mean any harm, he was just teasing her a little. Which had earned him a good slap from his mother, or rather two: "There, that one's for cussing, and one for pestering a girl. Don't you dare do that again!"

Immediately regretting her temper, Minnie took him in her arms. "I didn't hurt you, did I?" Harvey pretended to cry and they both ended up laughing at the melodrama of the situation. Intense and possessive like a real Jewish mother, Minnie had a soft spot for Harvey, her baby. She thought he was particularly charming and gentle compared to his older brother, who was more of a ruffian. Harvey also paid more attention to her. She was a fashion conscious, petite, curvy woman with curly brown hair and hazel eyes, and she liked it when Harvey gave her advice about her outfits. He had the sense of style to notice details his father or brother didn't even seem to see: a necklace she had just bought, a new dress, a different shade of lipstick. . . . At home as well, it was always Harvey who helped her the most, carrying her bags when she came back from the grocery store or volunteering to dry the dishes. Their closeness made Harvey feel proud, even if he sometimes felt a bit smothered—all the more so because he had a secret, and if his mother found out about it, she would be mortified. Maybe even love him less.

Lost in thought, it was some time before Harvey realized that police sirens were approaching Central Park, tearing through the peaceful, sunny Sunday atmosphere. He heard a few snatches of conversation: ". . . this way. . ."; ". . . there they are!"; ". . .caught in the act. . . ." By the time he realized that policemen were invading the lawn, he was already being hauled up from the ground and pushed towards a police car with blows from a baton.

Several other men were there who had been dragged towards the paddy wagons and hand-cuffed. One of them was bleeding profusely from his nose. Harvey gave him a handkerchief.

"It's terrible," his visibly shocked companion in misfortune whispered, "I don't know where we'll be able to go to have fun anymore, now that the police are coming after us everywhere, not just in our bars, but even in the park."

"Neither do I," Harvey replied, shaking from

head to foot. "Apparently the police raids are getting worse now. I even heard that if you get arrested you can end up with a police record stating you are a 'sexual delinquent.' Imagine what my poor mother would say! And it's not like we're doing anyone any harm, after all!"

"A while ago," the other man added, still badly upset, "someone told me about a guy the cops surprised with a lover. They immediately called his employer to tell them about his homosexuality. And do you know what happened? The poor guy was called into his boss's office, then committed suicide out of shame. It still makes me shudder."

Doubly stunned, by the blows from the batons and by this news, Harvey was trying to gather his wits when he saw a group of parents holding their children close, observing what was happening. Alerted by the shouts coming from the other side of the park, they had gathered to witness the scene of the arrests. Harvey especially noticed a father, also shirtless, holding his hands over his son's eyes, and shaking his head in disgust.

Before being thrown into the paddy wagon, he heard the man growl, "Go do your dirty business somewhere else, you degenerates, there are kids watching!" Were they going to release him with nothing more than a bruise on his forehead, or would they go through with their threat of telling his parents? More than anger, what Harvey was feeling was fear. Fear that his secret would be revealed in broad daylight to his family, his friends, his acquaintances, when he was only seventeen years old. For a long time now, Harvey had understood that he was not like the other boys, not like his brother, for example, who would ogle their neighbor Luisa's generous breasts and round behind. Harvey only had eyes for her brother James's blond curls.

He made sure he never showed his feelings in public, especially with his family around. Which didn't stop his mother from warning him one day about "those queer guys, called homosexuals, who hang around with other guys in some parts of town, in parks and bathhouses and bars." Minnie had felt compelled to add: "They are men that prefer to go out with other men, if you see what I mean. Sometimes they even go as far as dressing up as girls. That's why they're called fairies. They are sick, it's not their fault, but promise me you'll be careful."

She had put so much contempt and disgust into the word "fairies" that Harvey had understood only one thing: that he could never admit his homosexuality to his mother, for fear that she would die. And Harvey had always promised, in a fake light tone: "Don't worry, Mom, nothing will happen to me. I never hang out in those kinds of places anyway."

That day, in Central Park, the police had found no way to prove that Harvey's presence there was reprehensible or vulgar, and they had released him. But he kept the burning memory of that arrest branded in his memory.

Harvey had always felt different. And yet,

nothing in his appearance distinguished him from other boys. His physique was rather ordinary, except for his big nose, his giant feet, and his flappy ears which had earned him the nickname of "Pluto." Harvey had gotten used to this, especially since his friends would encourage him to play the class clown, which he happened to be very good at. He was only moderately interested in schoolwork, but had a talent for performing, especially standing up on the school desks and mimicking his teachers to his laughing classmates. And he loved football. All the swaggering around, but especially planning good plays and tactical alliances in order to win—that's what he liked. And on the football field, no one could call him a "pansy."

Not like Willy, that tall effeminate boy, who wore his shorts so tight they seemed ready to split at the seams at his slightest move. Willy walked with a swing in his hips even on the football field, laughed too loud, and would always purse his lips before saying anything. Poor Willy was openly mocked and bullied by their classmates, especially Glenn, who was both dumb and mean. Harvey could hardly hold himself back from smashing his fist into Glenn's nasty pimply face. One day, when Harvey was enraged by Glenn's vicious attitude to Willy, he played a practical joke on him. In the middle of a game, he pretended to have a sudden stomachache and went back to the locker room, where he took Glenn's clothes and hid them. Glenn had to walk home half naked from the stadium, hiding in all the doorways in the neighborhood on his way home. Served him right! Harvey was still laughing about it a week later. The football coach liked Harvey, although he did say he talked too much. "Be quiet, Milk, your loose tongue will get you into trouble one day."

His mother, however, sometimes worried that he wasn't "all there": "Where are you now, son?" . . . "What about now?" she would ask all day long. Which amused and endeared her to Harvey:

"With you, Mother dear," he would always

answer, then give her a hug and a kiss on the cheek.

In fact, what really set Harvey apart from all his classmates was his passion for opera. His mother was proud that, ever since he was sixteen, he would ask her for money, not to buy drink or shoes like the other boys his age, but for a ticket to the Saturday matinée at the Metropolitan Opera, the famous Met, on the corner of Broadway and 39th Street. From a very young age, Harvey had already had his favorite composers: Mahler, Strauss, Wagner, and the Italian composer of *La Traviata*, Giuseppe Verdi. But the one he loved best of all was Mozart, for the times he made the masters and servants sing together, like in *Don Giovanni*, his favorite opera.

For Harvey, the performance also took place in the auditorium, where he could sit back in his seat and admire the handsome guys in the audience. They would all be there, just as he was, to let themselves be carried away by the orchestra's music and the enchanting voices, but also to briefly touch hands, or smell a manly scent, or admire a strong chest under a tight shirt. More often than not, Harvey would be in good company after the show.

Morris Milk, Harvey's grandfather and a gentle, discreet man, understood and shared Harvey's love of classical music, though not of boys. The elderly man had no idea that his darling grandson was suffering from what he considered a "mental illness." One day, when his grandfather was having afternoon tea with Minnie, Harvey heard them comment on an article published in the *New York Times*:

"There's been another raid on a homosexual bar in Manhattan!" his grandfather exclaimed. "Those guys are dreadful, of course, but according to some famous physicians, homosexuality is a perversion that can be successfully treated."

"Oh yeah? How?" Minnie asked, with a touch of irony in her voice.

His mother seemed absolutely convinced that

being homosexual meant you were irredeemably deviant.

"It is entirely possible to convert homosexuals to heterosexuality, thanks to electroconvulsive therapy," Morris asserted with an air of authority.

"That it should come to this, really!" Minnie said in disgust.

2

In the Navy

On the college campus in Albany, the Jewish students did not mix with the other communities. Harvey did not think this was a good thing. He never missed an opportunity to make his disapproval known, even within his own group. Like the day when David, the president of Kappa Beta, the Jewish fraternity, refused to allow a gentile student to join. All David's friends had voted the same way: no. Except Harvey. When the result of the vote was announced, he stood up suddenly and left the university cafeteria, slamming the door on his way out, shouting: "Sure, practice the same discrimination as everybody else! That's what makes the world go round!"

Harvey was critical of other traditions too, such as hazing: "I award the laurels of stupidity to the idiot who invented this humiliating and dangerous ritual," he wrote in the college newspaper after a group of students forced new arrivals to dive naked into a freezing fountain one December morning. His loud voice and strong opinions were well-known all over the university, and it was therefore with a great sense of relief that the president of the university handed him his diploma on June 25, 1951.   That was a memorable day for Harvey, but also for his mother. Proudly looking on, sporting a fashionable blue dress and a fine new hairstyle, Minnie boisterously clapped and cheered for her genius son. So loudly that Harvey felt embarrassed. But he didn't want to spoil her happiness, especially knowing what he was going to announce to her that evening.

A few hours after the ceremony, Harvey's entire family gathered together: his grandfather, his father, his brother Bob with his fiancée, his mother and himself. Minnie had cooked a delicious Jewish meal: schnitzels, blintzes, a potato flour cake. . . . The dinner was a relaxed affair, Harvey was the king of the party, and glasses were clinking merrily. Up until the last moment, when Harvey tapped on the table lightly with a knife and asked for silence. His face suddenly shut down as he addressed his gathered family. He announced in a serious voice that he had taken the decision to enlist. In the Navy, in fact. His mother went as white as the immaculate tablecloth she had laid on the table in his honor. She opened her mouth to protest, but no sound came out. She remained immobile, as if paralyzed on her chair. His father was unable to utter a word either. It was his brother who finally exploded with rage:

"Are you out of your mind, to be even considering such a thing?"

"No, I am not out of my mind. It seems to me I could make myself useful by signing up. The communists are about to conquer South Korea.

You don't think I'm going to just stand there and let them get away with it, do you? Of course not!"

"America shed so much blood during the Second World War. That's enough war for now!"

"Maybe so, but my decision is final. I will enlist in the Navy, as our parents did before me, to defend liberty," Harvey retorted, holding Bob's angry gaze.

Then he went to his mother, and took her into his arms:

"Don't be angry with me, mother dear. I have to go, but I will come back in one piece, and just as handsome as ever, I promise . . . ."

And so Harvey set off on the *USS Kittiwake* from San Diego into the Pacific Ocean. He quickly rose through the ranks and became an officer, which gave him a privileged position in the military hierarchy and greater freedom of movement than others had. However, he continued to remain just as discreet about his sexual orientation, since anti-homosexual purges were frequent in the armed forces. This was confirmed by one of his gay companions during a boozy dinner at a bar at the San Diego military base:

"The Navy, just like all the other military corps, discharges homosexuals—even without any proof. We absolutely must remain silent about our private life, Harvey. Apparently quite a few of our kind committed suicide after being rejected by the army—as if we were unclean!"

"Well, in any case, I've had enough, I intend to leave. I've had to swallow all those insane sermons for almost four years now. I'm convinced that something better is waiting for me in civilian life. And you know, living in hiding all the time is starting to wear me down. We're not criminals!"

Harvey was forced to resign from the Navy in August 1955. As soon as he got back to New York, he started looking for work. After sending off a few applications, Harvey was hired as a math and history teacher at Hewlett High School near Woodmere. He got on well with the students, and his colleagues appreciated his dynamism. As a longstanding athlete, he offered to coach the school's basketball team, and that made him even more popular. The players went into battle twice a week facing other teams, often successfully, thanks to their new coach. Harvey was an indispensable player on a volleyball team with his own friends too. He had worked out a lot in the Navy and had kept his nimble reflexes, his keen sense of observation, and remarkable coordination. One day, however, Harvey's team lost when he was playing with them against the club team from City College.

"That's because of the handsome fifty-year-old playing like a god on the opposing team," Harvey tried to explain.

One of his teammates teased him:

"Come on, Harvey, if you keep playing, you'll be more attractive than he is in twenty years!"

"What? I'll never get to be that old. Ever since I was a kid, I had the premonition that something terrible is going to happen to me: I don't have much time. I have to live at a hundred miles an hour, because I'm going to die young, I know."

"Are you still alive, Harvey-the-champion-who-was-afraid-of-dying?"

Harvey immediately recognized the voice of his old friend. Fifteen years after their stinging defeat, the two men had just run into each other in the middle of Fifth Avenue. His old teammate had the same croaky voice and softness behind the eyes. Harvey hadn't changed either. Short and slim, with brown curly hair and the same energetic gait that had attracted his friend's attention. They celebrated meeting up again over a beer.

"Do you remember what you told me fifteen years ago?"

"Of course I do, and I still don't think I'll make old bones in this world. But that's enough about me. What are you up to these days?"

"I'm still at the same old job! I'm married and I have two children. What about you?"

"I left teaching. It was time for me to go do something else. I'm working in insurance now. A nice quiet job. I'm making more money, of course, but I wouldn't say I'm happier than when I was teaching. It's different, that's all."

Then Harvey added, taken by a sudden impulse:

"And if you ask me the name of my wife, I'll tell you I don't have one, and that I never will, because I'm a homosexual. Now you know everything."

His defiant expression and his clenched fists in his pockets did not escape his friend, who replied quickly:

"Hey, calm down, my friend. There are all kinds of people in this world. I knew from the first time we met that you weren't attracted to girls. You realize I couldn't care less about your sex life, right?"

"Thank you for your frankness and your friendship!" Harvey replied, shaking his hand warmly.

He is a good guy, Harvey said to himself as he walked home. *So not all men are against us then. But I could still never admit to my family who I really am. I'd rather die.*

Little did he know that a terrible twist of fate would stop him from revealing his secret.

The next day, he got a phone call from his brother: "Mother is dead, come quickly."

Harvey rushed to his mother's bedside. Minnie lay inert and pallid on her bed.

"She had a heart attack," his father sobbed when he saw Harvey.

"Can I have a moment alone with her?" Harvey asked, his face pasty white.

Behind the closed door, sitting beside his mother, Harvey cried for a long time, then gathered up his courage in both hands and finally confessed what he had never managed to tell her before. "You'll never, ever, be ashamed of me, I promise. I love you," he added, hugging her one last time. A whole part of his life was disappearing with Minnie's death. He was still overwhelmed when he left the room and felt his brother's heavy gaze upon him. Was he jealous? Unhappy? Had he heard what Harvey had said?

Harvey offered to take care of the funeral arrangements. He remembered that Minnie had once said, when they were talking about death together, that given the choice, she would prefer to be cremated despite the opposition of the traditional Jewish community. Keenly aware that he was about to shock his family and the entire Jewish community, Harvey took upon himself the decision to order a traditional white shroud to cremate his mother's body. His brother never forgave him: "It's blasphemy! I never want to see you again!"

The days following Minnie's death dragged for Harvey. He felt sad, and so profoundly alone. His latest boyfriend had just left him. There was nothing and nobody to keep him in New York anymore. His job was becoming a burden too, because his boss, William Ford, had been making unpleasant remarks about him for the last few weeks. This thin, balding man found a scapegoat in Harvey. One day he criticized him for being five minutes late, the next for making private phone calls at work. Not to mention his snide comments about Harvey's tight pants, his long hair. . . Harvey couldn't stand it anymore. One morning, Mr. Ford went too far: he called Harvey into his office, leaving the door wide open so that all his colleagues could hear, and yelled "Cut your hair, or resign!" Harvey saw red. He stood up suddenly, pushed over the desk, and slammed the door as he left his office, shouting "Yes, boss!" on the way out. He was immediately fired and had to leave his position that very day. As he closed the door to his office for the last time, he felt such an intense sense of freedom, as if someone had just taken him out of a strait-jacket.

3

From Manhattan to
San Francisco

On May 22, 1970, Harvey was taking a walk in
Manhattan, his nose in the air, his hands stuffed
into the pockets of his new jeans. He was whis-
tling and felt as light as the breeze ruffling his
hair. For his fortieth birthday that day, he had just
bought himself a whole new wardrobe, one that
was much more in the hippie fashion than his old
suits (which he ended up giving to the man who
lived outside on the street by his building). He was
looking fine in his colorful tee-shirt, with a scarf
tied around his neck, and brand-new sneakers.
New life, new look! he said to himself as he went
down into the subway at Christopher Street.

He was running down the steps two by two when his eyes met with those of a handsome young man with angelic hair and an athletic body. To think he might have missed such beauty! Harvey stopped short, enthralled by the princely yet gangly poise of the young man with emerald eyes. He forced him to slow down as he stared deep into his eyes and blurted out:

"Hi, my name is Harvey. Harvey Milk. I'm turning forty-one today, and I would love to spend the evening of my birthday with you."

"Joseph Scott Smith, twenty-two years old, my friends call me Scott," the handsome stranger said by way of introduction as he held out his hand and smiled, showing a row of perfect teeth. "I am honored by this unexpected proposition, and since I love surprises..."

"I take it you accept, then?"

"Let's just say I have nothing planned for tonight, so yes, I'll help you blow out your forty-one candles."

A few hours later, the champagne was flowing.

Harvey had just received his severance pay and had never felt happier. With Scott, maybe my life will take a different turn, he thought.

The days flew by. The two lovers were inseparable. They lived their romance in broad daylight, walking in the street holding hands, not caring that they could be insulted or arrested. It didn't matter anymore; Harvey was no longer scared. He did not want to hide any longer. And to prove to his new companion that he was proud of him and of their relationship, he suggested they go to the first Gay Pride march which was taking place on June 28, one year to the day after the Stonewall riots, named after the Stonewall Inn, where police had conducted a raid which degenerated into several days of violence against the gay community.

When the day came, Harvey and Scott left Washington Square at the corner of Sixth Avenue. The atmosphere was electric and the tension palpable among the demonstrators: word had gone round that the night before, five young gay men had been beaten up with baseball bats. Harvey and Scott marched in silence with other men under a banner saying, "GAY IS GOOD." The demonstration counted only a few people to begin with, but gradually got bigger and bigger, until over two thousand gays and lesbians joined the protestors. When they got to Central Park, they all started running at once, shouting "GAY POWER!" as loud as they could.

"We did it, Harvey," Scott whispered, with tears in his eyes. "We overcame our fears and came together in this incredible gathering. The first one in gay and lesbian history, but surely not the last. We should spare a thought for those who fought for us, some at the cost of their lives. It's because of them that we can march down the street with our heads held high as we did today."

"We should not have to put up with bullying and insults anymore. We must never again be ashamed of who we are. You know, I haven't achieved anything in my life that I am really proud of, but I can feel that things are changing now. I've got great ambitions for us. Let's leave New York. Let's go to San Francisco. It's a city with no taboos, a cultural melting pot, a place where oppressed minorities are welcome, whether they're ethnic or cultural."

It took two more years for their plans to leave to be realized, once the lovebirds had put together some savings. They decided to settle in the old working-class immigrant neighborhood of the Castro District, where gays could live in peace among a diverse multiracial population, and the hippies cared more about freedom and brotherhood than money and power.

"What will we do?" Scott had asked Harvey, stroking his curly hair, as they made their preparations.

"Nothing. Everything. I don't know yet, but we'll work it out together," Harvey replied, putting his arms around Scott.

The day of their departure finally arrived, and Harvey and Scott set off in their old apple-green '57 Chevy, which was covered in floral stickers.

"Let's hope it makes it!" Harvey sighed as he filled the trunk with their suitcases, a mattress and all his records. And it did make it. Several weeks and ten thousand miles later, Harvey and Scott got to the end of their journey with no mishaps. As soon as they arrived in San Francisco, they found a modest but charming one-bedroom apartment with a bay window and a view of Twin Peaks in the distance, on the top floor of a Victorian house at 575 Castro Street. For the first few months Harvey and Scott lived off their savings, footloose and carefree. During the day, they would explore the city, riding on its rickety trams, or briskly walking up and down its hills. They couldn't get enough of the sight of the Golden Gate Bridge, and spent hours strolling beside the ocean, along the sunny bay. Sometimes they went to the movies. The local Castro theater showed the kinds of films they liked. They loved their new city.

They realized that they would need to earn enough to get by. But how? They went through the want ads, met with a few recruiting agencies, all with no luck. One day, as they were starting to despair, Harvey had an inspiration:

"Scott, do you remember that camera film that the lab down the street returned to us last week?"

"Yeah, the messed up one where all the pictures were blurry and no good."

"Well, what if we opened our own photo processing shop? I've been thinking about it for a while. It doesn't seem that complicated and we will always do better than that place! The store at the bottom of our building is empty. Let's rent it!"

On March 3, 1973, Harvey and Scott opened their store, called Castro Camera. The day of the opening, several neighbors came in, to see what the store looked like, and especially to see the new owners, a gay couple. Another one in their neighborhood! Their first visitor was a pudgy man with fine lips and piggy eyes. Obviously ill at ease, he stood with his hands on his hips, shifting from one foot to the other. He stared at the sign, then at Harvey and Scott, who were looking magnificent in their black denim and flannel shirts, red for Harvey and yellow for Scott, before at last he asked:

"You're opening a store? You're a couple?"

"Sure are!" Harvey replied with enthusiasm, holding out his hand. The man barely touched it and then wiped his fingers with a handkerchief. Then he added, with disgust:

"Well then, I pray to God that you don't stay here too long. We believe in tradition and family values here."

Harvey and Scott watched him walk away, incredulous.

"Welcome to you too!" Scott called after him. Then to Harvey: "So this is your El Dorado?"

"Come on, don't let that idiot spoil such a wonderful day," Harvey replied, turning to the other visitors, who were all clearly more sympathetic and less hostile.

The months rolled by. Harvey and Scott met

more and more people, and the number of their customers grew day by day as well. But 575 Castro Street was not just a store. For many lost gays in the Castro, it became a place for meetings, discussions, sharing, and encounters. There was Mikael, who used to come there to rest, curled up for an hour or two on the soft couch in the store, because his parents had thrown him out. There was John, a mannered gay, who could forget, as he sipped a lemonade or a beer and listened to an operatic aria, that he couldn't find work because of his effeminate gait. There was William, always on the lookout for a kind word or a friendly gesture, who had tried several times to end his life because his lover had left him for another man. And Brian, Tom, Robert, Jude, and the rest, who came through the door of Castro Camera looking for advice, a smile, a contact. . . . That's when they weren't taking refuge at Harvey's place after being subjected to a homophobic assault. The outside world was still a place where violence toward gays prevailed.

"I was just followed by two guys. They kept punching me and called me a fairy," John once told Harvey as he rushed into the store. "Luckily I had my whistle on me, just like you said, the one we should wear and use to warn others if we are attacked. I whistled and whistled, then Richard—you know, the owner of the Elephant Walk bar, who's built like a ten-ton truck—came along and helped me get away. I got the worst fright of my life, I could see there were cops standing around, but they didn't even lift a pinkie finger to help me. Where would I be now if I didn't have that whistle on me?"

"Yeah, I can't stand seeing any more of these assaults go unpunished," Harvey replied as he wiped the blood off his young protégé's head. "I've had enough of our being arrested for 'disturbing the peace' or 'indecent behavior.' We have to fight to affirm our identity loud and clear, we can't be ashamed anymore, we have to come out of the closet!"

The young men around them that day all

clapped. *There's no doubt about it,* Scott mused with admiration, *Harvey has charisma. He is becoming the voice of all these oppressed people.* Scott turned towards his friend:

"You are a celebrity in our neighborhood now, and I know pretty soon I'm going to have to share you with all these people, and that makes me sad."

"Stop talking nonsense, Scott, my heart is yours forever and unconditionally. But you do have to admit that these guys need support. And not only them. All the residents and business owners in the neighborhood who come through our doors every day have the right to expect dignity and respect in their employment and daily lives. We must help them to be heard."

"Yeah, yeah, I know your speech: 'We will not win our rights by staying quietly in our closets. We are coming out to fight the lies, the myths, the distortions. I am tired of the conspiracy of silence. You must come out,'" Scott replied, looking pensive all of a sudden. Stuck on the store windows were flyers Harvey had pasted up for upcoming demonstrations by political, ecological, and local interest groups; on the counter there were piles of petitions to sign. That day, Harvey had an important announcement to make; he got out a table and climbed up onto it. There was a new sparkle in his eyes. His hair was tied up in a ponytail, he cleared his throat, grabbed a bullhorn, and proclaimed in a solemn, almost theatrical voice:

"Let's go back to the beginning. I am announcing my candidacy for Supervisor of a great City. Think about that for a moment. A city isn't a collection of buildings—it isn't downtown with the B of A and a TransAmerica Tower, it isn't the parking lots or the freeways or the theatres or the massage parlors. A city is people. In this case, some 675,000. Some 60,000 of them live in District 5. They're Latin and Black, white and Chinese, young and old, straight—and gay.

Each of those people has his or her own hopes and aspirations, his or her own viewpoints and problems. Each of them contributes something unique to the life of the city. Friends talking across fences, the baseball players in the playground on Sunday, old ladies tottering down the street hand-in-hand, the smile from a passing stranger."*

The Mayor of Castro, as Harvey called himself, received enthusiastic applause from the crowd that had gathered around him. However, despite this successful first public declaration, and a very active political campaign in the Castro, he was beaten. He studied the reasons for his failure with his team for several days, then one morning sent everyone packing. He needed to be alone with Scott—it was becoming such a rare occurrence! They went out together to roam the streets of San Francisco.

That stroll turned out to be an expensive one: Scott bought Harvey a tape-recording deck—"to record your memoirs," he said—and Harvey

---

* The actual words that Harvey spoke that day have not survived, but these are the words he spoke with a similar sentiment when he announced his third run for Supervisor in 1977.

bought a VCR, one of the first videocassette players. They spent the evening watching old movies, snuggled together eating marshmallows. As Harvey laid there with Scott, he couldn't stop thinking about his next move. He imagined himself gathering the press, and exclaiming: "From now on, you will have to deal with me in our city's political landscape and nationwide too. My name is Harvey Milk, I am gay and proud to be so. I am here to fight for our rights to be recognized. Just like you, I want to live a normal life."

4

"My Name Is Harvey Milk"

In 1975, Harvey's name was on the ballot again in the San Francisco Board of Supervisors elections. He lost for the second time, but gained more votes, though not from some moderate gays more inclined towards assimilation who believed that he gave them a poor image. They were in favor of discretion, and totally rejected Harvey's calls for gays to come out of hiding. His change from his hippie wardrobe to a three-piece suit had not convinced his detractors, nor had his shorter haircut. Harvey was exasperated by this rejection from a significant part of the San Francisco gay community. One day, as he was leaving a stormy meeting with a group of "Aunt Marys," as he called them, he went into Elephant Walk for a talk with the bar owner Richard. He was flushed with anger, his hair sticking out and his tie askew, and banged on the table:

"I'm fighting sixteen hours a day for guys who don't even dare stand up for themselves and prefer to hide, when they should be fighting for their rights!"

"Be patient, Harvey, you'll win in the end, even if you have to wait ten years."

"I don't have that long. I'll never be an old man. My time is short, I know that. I need to reach my goals quickly."

"Come on, Harvey! I just heard you rallied one of the three most macho unions in town to our cause—the firefighters!"

"Well, they're guys just like us, or almost like us at least," Harvey explained, suddenly calmer.

He had taken off his jacket, opened up his top shirt button, and was feeling much better after losing his temper. He continued:

"They all just want to live in peace with their

families. I suggested in my campaign that they should be able to stop work at four o'clock on Fridays. George Moscone, you know, the former senator of California, who was just elected Mayor of San Francisco partly thanks to my support, promised that he would agree to my demands. I've been the firefighters' god ever since," Harvey added, puffing out his chest. He led his friend to the bar's window front:

"Here, take a look."

Richard could not believe his eyes: at the other end of the street were two virile firefighters perched up on an extendable ladder sticking Harvey's new campaign poster up on a wall.

Harvey and Richard burst out laughing.

"Thanks to you, I've seen everything in this town!"

Harvey was heading to a meeting with Mayor Moscone, so he straightened his pants, tied up his tie again, and smoothed down his unruly hair with some water. His reflection in the mirror matched the image he wanted the mayor to see:

a bold, committed activist who was both present-able and credible. Everything was going well so far, and the two men liked each other. Harvey thought Moscone was open-minded, intelligent, and trustworthy; Moscone considered Harvey's frankness and no-nonsense approach to be valuable political assets. *This bodes well for the future*, Harvey thought as he vigorously shook the mayor's hand.

After this second defeat, Harvey got back to work immediately. He held political meetings during the day and wrote speeches at night, covering pages and pages with ink. Then he rehearsed them, either alone in his apartment, or in the store, surrounded by his team. Some rallies took place in the street. Standing up high on a podium, his arm raised and pointing his finger, Harvey would address the crowd, starting all of his speeches with the same striking words: "My name is Harvey Milk and I'm here to recruit you." Harvey was so absorbed by his political activity that he neglected Scott more and more, to the point where Scott felt like just another pawn in the game—the most insignificant pawn of all, in fact. And politics, discrimination, violence, problems . . . he just couldn't take it anymore. One morning, gathering up his courage, he joined Harvey in the kitchen where, for once, he was having breakfast sitting at the table with a newspaper open before him. Scott sat down across from him with tears in his eyes, and in a voice full of emotion announced he was leaving. Harvey jumped up but was incapable of saying anything in response. His hands suddenly started shaking. Scott came around the table and took him in his arms, whispering:

"You were my whole life, my mentor, my strength. Today we are parting ways. Your path is clear, you will go far. And I might slow you down with my doubts and fears. I will always love you. Goodbye."

He pulled away from his partner and left without turning back, leaving Harvey standing in the middle of the kitchen, empty-handed and staring into the void, his coffee cup smashed on the floor where it had fallen out of his hands. Harvey slammed the door that Scott had left open, as hard as he could. The ceiling light swayed but Harvey didn't care. He put on *Carmen* at full volume, then *Don Giovanni*. Opera had always soothed him. But this time, the magic didn't work. Harvey spent all day pacing around the apartment, then threw himself onto his bed, his nose buried in the sheets that still smelled of Scott. He slept terribly that night, with nightmares where Scott and Minnie seemed to blend into one person. At last, at daybreak, when the moon finally disappeared from the horizon, he took a shower, shaved closely, put on his best suit, and left the apartment. He went down into the store where his friends were already waiting for him, despite the early hour. John offered him a cup of strong coffee and made the V for victory sign with his fingers: "Everything is OK, Harvey, we're here if you need us." Harvey didn't have time to answer before the phone rang. He dashed to pick up the receiver, hoping that it was Scott and that he had changed his mind. But what he heard made his blood run cold:

"Hello Harvey, my name is David, I'm seventeen and I live in Phoenix. I wanted to tell you how much I admire you, and that I would support you if I could. But the thing is, my parents have just found out that I'm gay, and they're taking me to hospital tomorrow because they want to have what they call my 'unnatural deviance' treated. I'm scared. I want to die."

"No!" Harvey shouted into the phone. "Listen to me, David, get onto a train, a plane or a bus right now, and head straight for a big city, New York, San Francisco, anywhere. . . . Come join us. Don't let them do that to you. You have nothing to be ashamed of, you have done nothing wrong. Don't let them get the better of you."

"I know," the teenager replied, sobbing, "but I can't move, I'm disabled, I'm in a wheelchair. . . ."

Then the line went dead. Harvey shook the handset and banged on the switch several times, nothing worked. He sat slumped in front of the telephone for a long time, feeling upset and powerless at what he had just heard. "Without hope, life isn't worth living," he repeated several times. Then he stood up: "Our fight must go on, now more than ever."

5

A Victory for Gay Rights

"I'd like to introduce Anne Kronenberg, my new campaign manager!" Harvey declared to his team.

The group of men turned to look at a short blonde woman aged twenty-three. She appeared timid and reserved at first, and was one of the first women ever to appear in the place! But Anne rolled up her sleeves, put her fists on her hips and, paying no attention to the astounded stares of the men, roared in an ironic voice:

"You're not afraid of women, are you? Or lesbians, right? Well then, hello everyone, and let's get to work, shall we?"

"At your service, boss!" Harvey shouted with a dramatic swing of his hips. Then he added through pursed lips and with his pinky in the air: "My poor dear, I pity you with all these men!" That little performance led to general hilarity, and everyone set back to work in a good mood, following Harvey's lead. Just like every other day, he had woken up at 5:30 and gone out to meet people at bus stops, in coffee shops, in stores. . . . He would start a conversation with anyone, young, old, Black, white, Asian, Latinx. . . and talk to them about hope, life, and love. Then he would rush off at a run to a political meeting, before returning to his headquarters around midnight to help the volunteers stuff envelopes. Nothing could stop him, not even the many death threats he received. He would read them aloud and stick them on the refrigerator. "Which one do you think is the best one?" he would ask Anne, sardonically. She was terrified and begged him to call the police. "The police? They would be only too pleased to get rid of an agitator like me!"

"Well, at least don't stand on that podium anymore, you are too exposed up there," she pleaded before he made one of his speeches. But Harvey wouldn't listen and only increased the number of his public appearances.

And he finally won. At forty-seven years of age, he was at last elected to the Board of Supervisors of San Francisco, on George Moscone's team. He shared that role with others, including one Dan White, a former city firefighter who had retired to devote himself to local politics. "A city fire-fighter?" Harvey wondered, as he shook hands with a tall well-built man, with a square chin and a wide forehead. . . . Yes, it was in fact the same firefighter who had stuck up his posters a few months earlier! Harvey wanted to thank him for his contribution to the campaign, but Dan inter-rupted him, his jaw clenched:

"The thing is, you should never have been allowed to be here in the first place. And I will never forget the humiliation of having to stick up a poster for a sick man like you!"

Then he disappeared before Harvey could say

a single word. Harvey leaned towards Anne and whispered:

"That man is openly homophobic and clearly set against me. He can't stand the fact that a gay man could represent his country. The game isn't over, darling, but this is a first step towards victory."

"Well, let's celebrate then!"

That night, Harvey's headquarters was the place to be. A crowd of people came to congratulate the hero of the hour. Harvey, with stars in his eyes and a triumphant smile on his lips, first thanked each member of his team for their commitment and devotion:

"This is not my victory, it's yours and yours and yours."

Then he turned to the group of admirers who were waiting for him outside and they all started a march towards City Hall. They walked all the way down Castro Street to the Castro Theater at the corner of Market Street, where other groups joined them. The procession got bigger and bigger, and when it finally arrived at City Hall there were thousands of people singing, dancing, embracing. Harvey was surrounded by a euphoric crowd. He pulled away from the group and stood in front of the beautiful white building, then bowed and addressed the crowd:

"If a gay can win, it means that there is hope that the system can work for all minorities if we fight."

A volley of applause greeted him.

From the very next day, Dan White's hostility was obvious. As they passed each other in a hallway, Dan pretended to ignore Harvey, but the situation was delicate: Harvey was with Dan's secretary Sally. He couldn't very well ignore the young woman only because she was walking alongside Harvey. Dan mumbled:

"Hello Sally, hi Harvey."

Harvey laughed, "Hello, my dear Dan, how are you doing today? Did you enjoy that historic moment, our victory?"

The secretary, who could see what was going on, escaped on the pretext of having to mail a letter, leaving the two men face to face. Dan hissed:

"You can be smart, but I will not let myself be chased out of San Francisco by social deviants, by immoral basket cases like you. Society does not exist without the family, whatever you like to say, Harvey Milk."

"Oh, I have nothing against families, believe me. And I'm here to convince you that we are not what you think we are," Harvey retorted, before adding with a wide smile, "Say hi to your wife and kids!"

When he got back to his headquarters from City Hall, Harvey told Anne about his encounter. She was horrified by what Dan had said.

"That guy frightens me. Be careful, Harvey. Maybe he's the one sending you death threats!"

"No, he's not, he's just stupid, that's all. And he's a Catholic extremist, it's no surprise that he has prejudices about homosexuals. Don't worry, I'll look after him."

In the days following the election, Harvey received thousands of letters of congratulations, and two telegrams that warmed his heart. First, a short one from Scott: "Congratulations, Harvey. You won. I knew it." His old volleyball teammate also wrote to him, warmly, as usual: "Harvey, my friend, you had a dream, and you made it come true."

The press asked him for interviews, including the *Bay Area Reporter*, to which he gave an exclusive:

> *"I am just a figurehead, the one who happened to step out of the back room. I am the one who happens to have done it. It is your victory, and I do not mean just the ones who worked and voted for me. . . The opponents threw everything against us—innuendos, phony endorsements, and all—and we still won."*

He also explained his motivation to run initially:

"When the mayor asked me a year ago what my motivation was, I told him that I remember what it was like to be 14 and Gay. I know that somewhere today there is a 14-year-old child who discovers that he or she is Gay and learns that the family may throw that child out of the house. The police will harass that child. The state will say that the child is a criminal. . . . Maybe that child read in the newspaper, 'Homosexual Elected in San Francisco,' and that child has two options: move to San Francisco or stay in San Antonio or Des Moines and fight. The child has hope."

Harvey also continued to receive insulting messages and hate mail. He joked that his favorite one was, "Milk you faggot, you didn't win anything except the right to get your brains blown out!"

The day he received it, he shrugged and adopted a relaxed attitude. And yet that evening he couldn't get to sleep. He got up again, pulled on a sweater, fixed himself a whole pot of coffee, and sat down at his kitchen table with his Dictaphone. Then he pressed the recording button: "My name is Harvey Milk. . . ." All night, he spoke into the microphone and filled three cassette tapes with a will which he titled "Political Will." He talked in a soft but firm voice about his years of struggle and political activism, his coming out, his determination to change people's fundamental ideas. He also explained how a gay rights activist as popular as he was could represent a threat to a disturbed person. Then he put the tapes away at the back of his wardrobe and went back to bed, his mind at rest.

Harvey had just had a genius idea. He set it out to his staff:

"The President of the United States himself must listen to us. He is taking an official trip to California, so I invited him to City Hall with his wife. He'll be coming tomorrow. I need a photographer to immortalize our handshake so that it can be on the front page of all the papers. Imagine a US president shaking a gay man's hand!"

As planned, the following day Jimmy Carter and his wife arrived at City Hall. They visited various offices, accompanied by the supervisors. The president greeted several people, and then he found himself face to face with Harvey. Embarrassed, he walked around him, crossed his arms . . . until finally Harvey, guessing the reason for his discomfort and keen to get it over and done with, took the president's hand between his, and faced the photographer, saying: "Smile, Mr. President!"

Harvey had succeeded. The photograph of Jimmy Carter shaking an openly gay politician's hand was all over the country by the next day. And it would, Harvey hoped, serve his next goal: to convince homosexuals that they could come out without risking losing their jobs. Mayor Moscone, who supported Harvey in this project, instituted a city ordinance which forbade any discrimination based on sexual orientation. He was trying, in his way, to counter Proposition 6, which was aimed at terminating the employment of homosexuals in public schools. A vast anti-gay campaign was rocking the country and Harvey had to confront several homophobic extremists who were in favor of Proposition 6: Dan White, but also others like Anita Bryant. She was a second-rate singer, and the head of a political organization called Save the Children. She railed against Moscone's project: "If we give civic rights to homosexuals, then why not to prostitutes and thieves?"

Day after day, Harvey defended his position in front of journalists, at street rallies, on TV, at the barber's, the food market, in bars. With his fist held high and a determined look in his eyes, he tirelessly repeated: "People are tired of talking about taxes and Jarvis-Gann. People will also get tired of talking about Briggs and gay rights. To these people, I say that the day we stop talking about gay rights is the day we no longer have them." He went so far as to call on the president again: "Jimmy Carter, you talk about human rights a lot; in fact, you want to be the world's leader for human rights. Well, damn it, lead! There are some fifteen to twenty million lesbians and gay men in this nation listening very carefully. Jimmy Carter, when are you going to talk about THEIR rights?" Then he wrote a long speech for Gay Pride, which was to be on June 25, 1978.

"This will be my final blow to all those extremists!" he announced to Anne triumphantly, before climbing onto the podium to address several thousand people: "Gay people are painted as child molesters. I want to talk about that. I want to talk about the myth of child molestations by Gays. I want to talk about the fact that in this state some 95% of child molestations are heterosexual and usually committed by a parent. That all child abandonments are heterosexual. That all abuse of children is by their heterosexual parents. That some 98% of the six million rapes committed annually in this country are heterosexual. That one out of every three women who will be murdered in this state this year will be murdered by their husbands. That some 30% of all heterosexual marriages contain domestic violence. Gay brothers and sisters, what are you going to do about it? You must come out. Come out to your parents, your relatives. I know that it is hard and that it will hurt them, but think of how they will hurt you in the voting booth! Come out to your friends, if indeed they are your friends. . . . Break down the myths; destroy the lies and distortions for your own sake, for their sake, for the sake of the youngsters who are being terrified by the votes coming from Dade County to Eugene!" he concluded, waving the new multicolor flag that he had asked his friend, the artist Gilbert Baker, to make for him.

That symbol of the gay and lesbian community was floating in the blue sky of San Francisco. The audience was gazing up at it with shining eyes. The atmosphere was tense, because everyone knew that their lives could be ruined if Proposition 6 passed. Some faces bore traces of fear and exhaustion, but they were all touched to the heart, for they knew that thanks to Harvey, the course of history might be changing.

And they were right. On November 7, 1978, Proposition 6 was rejected by a resounding vote of 59 to 41 percent. All through San Francisco a delirious crowd made up of gays and lesbians, Black and white, young and old gathered at City Hall, chanting: "Harvey Milk, we won! Harvey Milk, thank you!" Then the group left and marched through the streets all day, bearing banners that said, "I'm gay, so what?" Others walked in silence, holding lit candles.

Harvey was mad with joy. He had fought like a lion against the worst humiliation anyone could know: having to lie about who you really are. His best reward was a phone call he received after his victory was announced in the media:

"Harvey, I wanted to congratulate you, but especially to say thank you. I escaped, just like you advised me to. I left my parents and I'm now living far away from them. I'm doing well. Thank you once again."

Harvey recognized the voice, it was David, the teenager who had called him several months ago, on the brink of suicide. Harvey was overwhelmed with emotion:

"Thanks to you, and congratulations for your courage! By acting as you did, you're proving to the whole world that we are right to smash down the closet doors."

Three days after this victory for gay rights, Dan White resigned from his position as city supervisor in anger and humiliation. He claimed he wanted to spend more time with his newborn child, after the long and difficult period he had devoted to politics. However, several days later, Dan White insisted on being reinstated. He telephoned George Moscone several times, tried to get a meeting with him, all to no avail. The mayor remained unresponsive to his demands and explained this to Harvey: "If that supporter of

Proposition 6 returns, he will hate us. All White had to do was do his job. But he decided to put an end to his political career, so let him stay in civilian life!" Harvey was relieved. He didn't see that anything good would come of Dan White's return.

Moscone planned to announce his rejection of White's request at a press conference on the morning of November 27. At 10:00 a.m., dressed in a rumpled suit, unshaven and with puffy eyes, Dan White entered City Hall through a first-floor window. He climbed the three floors that led to office 317, Mayor Moscone's. Once there, he requested an appointment through the mayor's assistant, and was granted one, soon entering Moscone's office alone. At the sight of White, Moscone jumped up and yelled:

"What are you doing here, Dan?"

"Let me come back," he mumbled, but then, understanding that it was too late, he took a revolver out of his pocket and shot two bullets into the mayor's head.

Moscone collapsed inert on the carpet, which was soon covered by a crimson puddle. Dan left the office, looking stunned. He climbed the stairs four at a time to Harvey's office. After pulling Milk aside and exchanging a few words, White shot his longtime enemy five times. Harvey Milk fell dead, his eyes wide open on his assassin.

The first openly gay American politician, who had devoted much of his life to defending the rights of homosexuals and other minorities, and to the respect of difference, had been savagely assassinated.

At the end of his recorded will, he had said, "If a bullet should enter my brain, let that bullet destroy every closet door."

Afterword: They Too Said No

Homophobia literally means "the fear of homo-sexuals." In practice, it is a set of negative beliefs, behaviors, laws, and societal norms that work to discriminate against people who are lesbian, gay, bisexual, or transgender (LGBT). This form of oppression based on sexual orientation often stems from religious extremism or conservative political beliefs. It can be disguised as "humor" (making fun of someone's gender identity) or self-hate (often termed "internalized homopho-bia"). It can feel like invisible pressures to have children or ostracization from community groups and family homes. It can also take the form of physical or verbal violence (also known as "gay bashing"), housing and job discrimination, police brutality, or laws governing what you can wear and how you can have sex.

No one has a right to control who you love. Silence is easy. But we can also be brave and refuse homophobia each day. People engage in this fight in big and small ways: from marching to mourning, from political education to poetry, from simple acts of care to moving in solidarity with other marginalized groups.

After Harvey's death, the people of San Francisco paid their respects to their assassinated elected officials with a candlelit march through the whole city at nightfall. The newspaper headlines read: "The city weeps." However, from the very beginning of Dan White's trial, five months after the murders, anger started to rise among Milk and Moscone's supporters, and in other citizens as well. From the start of the proceedings, the jurors were on Dan White's side. None of them were homosexual or racial minorities, or held progressive political opinions. Even though

Dan White was found guilty and responsible for the crime at the time, he was sentenced to only seven years in prison. A demonstration was organized in front of City Hall, which rapidly turned into a riot. Dan White spent only five and a half years in prison. He committed suicide in 1985.

In the 1970s, when Harvey was elected to office, homosexual relations were still against the law. Same-sex couples could not marry and people who liked to "cross-dress" (wear clothes that did not "match" their perceived gender) were frequently arrested. The AIDS epidemic was rapidly approaching, a public health crisis that would kill hundreds of thousands of LGBT people simply because the government did not care enough to find a treatment for the deadly virus. In that political climate, Harvey's murder quickly became a symbol of the ways the United States fails to value and protect gay life. But Harvey's courage to live as himself is also symbolic of the power gay people have to resist.

Perhaps the most famous incident of collective action against homophobia occurred just a few years before Harvey's death. In the early hours of June 28, 1969, New York City police raided the Stonewall Inn, a gay bar located on Christopher Street in Manhattan's Greenwich Village. At a time when it was still illegal to serve alcohol to so-called "sexual deviants," Stonewall was a haven for gays, drag queens and kings, and homeless LGBT youth. Police raids on gay bars were common at the time. Yet that morning something was different. Fed up with constant social discrimination and police harassment, iconic transgender activist Marsha "Pay It No Mind" Johnson, along with her friends Sylvia Rivera and Stormé DeLarverie, decided to fight back. As the legend goes, someone threw a brick at a police officer and a riot erupted, leading to six days of protests by hundreds of angry gays.

The Stonewall uprising marked the beginning of a bold gay rights movement throughout the US and around the world. On the one-year anniversary of the riots, thousands of people, including

Harvey and Scott, marched in the streets of Manhattan for the first Gay Pride parade. The crowd's official chant was "Say it loud, gay is proud." Eight years later, for the Gay Pride march of 1978, the rainbow flag, the symbol of the LGBT community, was created thanks to artist Gilbert Baker and the legacy of Harvey Milk. The flag was first designed in eight colors (pink, red, orange, yellow, green, turquoise, indigo and violet), then appeared without the pink because that dye color was not readily available for mass production, then without the turquoise, on the occasion of Harvey's death. During the memorial procession, the flag needed to be cut in half in order to be flown on either side of the street, and for that an even number of colors was required: red, orange, yellow, green, indigo, and violet.

Since then, LGBT people have continued to risk their lives to say no to homophobia in whatever form it takes. Escaping to San Francisco just a few years after Harvey did, Lou Sullivan was the first openly gay transgender man that we know of. Through his writings and community organizing, Lou taught us that sexual orientation and gender identity are separate—an act of bravery at a time when medical authorities denied that possibility. Communist activist Leslie Feinberg lived a fearless life, too. Leslie's 1993 book *Stone Butch Blues* is an irreplaceable record of lesbian life before the Stonewall riots. Lawyer and civil rights activist Pauli Murray courageously taught us that sexual orientation, race, and gender all interact to oppress different LGBT people in different ways. Saying no to homophobia, Pauli insisted, means saying no racism and sexism just as loudly.

Today, a majority of Americans say they have relatives and friends who are lesbian, gay, bisexual, or transgender. From television to books to movies, LGBT people are increasingly visible and positively represented in popular culture. Laws prohibiting homosexual relations have been struck down and gay people have gained the right to marry as well as adopt children in all 50 states. Thanks to the work of grassroots organizations like ACT UP (AIDS Coalition to Unleash Power), HIV treatment is readily available. In August 2009, forty years after his death, Harvey Milk was posthumously awarded the Presidential Medal of Freedom, one of the highest civil distinctions in the United States, by President Barack Obama.

Still, rights are won, and rights are lost. Forty-four years after Harvey's death, LGBT people continue to face religious persecution, housing insecurity, inaccessible medical care, and high levels of unemployment. And, like Pauli taught us, different members of the LGBT community continue to experience homophobia in different ways. From housing to healthcare to hate crimes, Black and brown transgender people bear the brunt of anti-gay violence. During the 2022 legislative season, dozens of states put forth homophobic bills which specifically target transgender youth. In many countries, homosexual acts themselves are severely penalized by law:

life imprisonment, deportation, corporal punishment, forced labor, and even the death penalty. The battle is far from won.

In 2010, President Barack Obama repealed the "Don't ask, don't tell" law that forbade US Army recruiters and personnel from asking applicants and members about their sexual orientation but also barred openly gay people from serving in the military. Servicemembers were thus forced to stay in the closet or face immediate discharge. For many, the right to openly serve was a major victory. Since 1994, more than 13,000 soldiers had been discharged due to the application of "Don't ask, don't tell." Other gay rights activists have pointed out that refusing homophobia is part of a much bigger picture.

Himself a veteran, Harvey believed that anti-war activism was directly connected to the fight for gay liberation. In 1955, after joining the Navy during the Korean War, Milk was discharged on account of his sexual orientation. As part of this dismissal, he was reportedly forced to describe the sex he had

had while serving in the military in a 152-page document—an attempt to humiliate him even further. In the following years, Harvey became increasingly opposed to military action. He regularly demonstrated against the Vietnam War and was fired from one of his many jobs for burning his Bank of America card in protest of the US invasion of Cambodia. Throughout his life, Milk was a vocal opponent of antisemitism too. He knew, of course, that gay and transgender people, along with Jews, were persecuted by the Nazi regime during the Holocaust. Saying no to homophobia, Harvey insisted, means saying no to all forms of oppression: no to war, no to racism, and no to fascism.

Throughout history there have been societies that respected and honored people of all different sexual orientations and gender identities. To say no to homophobia is to remember that we have the power to recreate a culture centered around autonomy, courage, and justice.

Building a world where we can safely be ourselves is a community effort. It might look like remaining fearless in the face of violence, as Marsha and Sylvia did. Or fighting against housing and employment discrimination like Leslie. Or helping to organize community events, for example clothing swaps or LGBT picnics, like Lou.

This fight also happens in everyday decisions and ordinary acts of care. Speaking up when a friend uses "gay" as an insult. Educating ourselves on the history of homophobia, and questioning stereotypes in movies and books. Asking the LGBT people in our lives how best to support them—and always, *always* respecting their decision about when to come out.

If you are the victim of homophobia, resistance can simply mean choosing to love yourself rather than internalize whatever has been done to you. That might mean reaching out to a trusted adult or finding a safe space online to talk to an LGBT peer. It might mean investing in little acts of self-care, like a bubble bath or movie night.

We all have the right to live free of discrimination, bullying, and harassment. You should never have to fight alone. To say no to homophobia is what we all must do so that we can live freely and fully. To say no to homophobia is to choose love. To live out and proud, like Harvey did.

Chronology

May 22, 1930: Harvey Bernard Milk is born in Woodmere, New York.

June 28, 1969: The Stonewall Riots begin when New York City police raid the Stonewall Inn in Greenwich Village. The following six days of protest galvanize the gay rights movement.

June 28, 1970: On the anniversary of Stonewall, thousands of people march in streets for the first "gay liberation march," what we now celebrate as Pride.

1972: Harvey Milk moves to San Francisco, like many homosexuals at that time, and settles in the Castro District.

1973 and 1975: Harvey Milk runs unsuccessfully for the office of City Supervisor, and is nick-named the Mayor of Castro Street, with wide support from the homosexual community.

1977: Harvey Milk is elected as a representative of the 5th district of San Francisco and becomes the first openly homosexual man elected to public office in the Unites States. During the eleven months he had in office, he took action to protect gay rights and opposed Proposition 6, a law that would have authorized the firing of openly homosexual teachers. Thanks to his efforts, this law was not adopted.

November 27, 1978: Harvey Milk and the Mayor of San Francisco George Moscone are assassi-nated. The murderer, Dan White, is sentenced to only seven years in prison. The verdict leads to violent riots.

For More Information

HELPLINES AND RESOURCES:
The Trevor Project: the world's largest suicide prevention and crisis intervention organization for LGBT youth. (212) 695-8650; trevorproject.org
Trans Lifeline: a grassroots hotline run by and for trans people. (877) 565-8860; translifeline.org
Sylvia Rivera Law Project: a legal aid organization serving low-income people and people of color who are transgender. (212) 337-8550; srlp.org
Q Chat Space: a digital center for LGBT teens to connect in professionally facilitated discussion groups. qchatspace.org
Scarleteen: an inclusive and supportive relationships and sexual education resource for teens. scarleteen.com
Find your local LGBT community center: lgbtcenters.org
You Know, Sex, Cory Silverberg and Fiona Smyth, 2022.
Hello, Cruel World: 101 Alternatives to Suicide for Teens, Freaks, and Other Outlaws, Kate Bornstein, 2006.

BOOKS:

Bitter, Akwaeke Emezi, 2022; *Pet*, Akwaeke Emezi, 2021.

Out of Salem, Hal Schrieve, 2019.

Harvey Milk: His Lives and Death, Lillian Faderman, 2018.

Fierce Femmes and Notorious Liars, Kai Cheng Thom, 2016.

An Archive of Hope: Harvey Milk's Speeches and Writings, ed. Jason Edward Black and Charles E. Morris, 2013.

The Pink Triangle: The Nazi War Against Homosexuals, Richard Plant, 2011.

The Mayor of Castro Street: The Life & Times of Harvey Milk, Randy Shilts, 2008.

The Dictionary of Homophobia: A Global History of Gay & Lesbian Experience, ed. Louis-Georges Tin, 2008.

The Faggots & Their Friends Between Revolutions, Larry Mitchell and Ned Asta, 1977.

Giovanni's Room, James Baldwin, 1956.

WATCH:

Heartstopper, Euros Lyn, 2022.

Steven Universe, Rebecca Sugar, 2013.

575 Castro St., Jenni Olson, 2013: vimeo.com/152913341.

How to Survive a Plague, David France, 2012.

Milk, Gus Van Sant, 2009.

Paris is Burning, Jennie Livingston, 1991.

Tongues Untied, Marlon Riggs, 1989.

The Times of Harvey Milk, Rob Epstein, 1984.

Discussion Questions

Have you ever said "no" to homophobia? In what circumstances? Have you ever witnessed homophobia and stayed quiet? What might you do differently in the future?

In anticipation of his murder, Harvey famously said, "If a bullet should enter my brain, let that bullet destroy every closet door." What is so powerful about deciding to live "out and proud"? Why might some people not want—or be able—to do so?

After his death, Harvey became a martyr for the gay rights movement. What did his assassination mean for the gay community, both in symbolic and material terms? Did Harvey have to die to prove his humanity?

What similarities and/or differences do you see between the gay rights movement of the 70s and the fight for queer liberation today?

How is the fight for gay rights connected to the fight for all human rights? In your discussion, consider Harvey's anti-war activism and Jewish identity. You might also consider figures such as Marsha P. Johnson and Lou Sullivan.

What does "pride" mean to you?

About the Author and Translator

Having often seen the ravages of intolerance towards homosexuals through her work as a journalist, SAFIA AMOR swore that she would do what she could to fight it. This first novel rendering justice to a genuine anti-homophobic activist is part of that goal.

RUTH DIVER has translated works by several of France's leading contemporary novelists, including *The Little Girl on the Ice Floe* by Adélaïde Bon, *The Revolt* by Clara Dupont-Monod, and *Arcadia* by Emmanuelle Bayamack-Tam. Her translation of *Maraudes* by Sophie Pujas won the 2016 Asymptote Close Approximations Fiction Prize.

NEW AND FORTHCOMING
THEY SAID NO TITLES

Mordechai Anielewicz: No to Despair by Rachel Hausfater

Anna Politkovskaya: No to Fear by Dominique Conil

Víctor Jara: No to Dictatorship by Bruno Doucey

Rosa Luxembourg: No to Borders by Anne Blanchard

Chico Mendes: No to Deforestation by Isabelle Collombat

Léonard Peltier: No to the Massacre of Indigenous Peoples by Elsa Solal

Primo Levi: No to Forgetting by Daniele Aristarco and Stéphanie Vailati

Aimé Césaire: No to Humiliation by Nimrod

Janusz Korczak: No to Contempt for Childhood by Isabelle Collombat

George Sand: No to Prejudice by Ysabelle Lacamp

Victor Hugo: No to the Death Penalty by Murielle Szac